The Trouble with Gran

Babette Cole

COLLINS
PICTURE LIONS

The trouble with Gran is . . .

None of the other OAP's suspected a thing . . .

. . . until our teacher tried to organise an outing for them, to Wethorp, as our school project!

"But we want to go somewhere hot and exciting!" said Gran.

"Sit down and be quiet!" snapped teacher.

Wethorp was awful.

Gran started to play up!

We went to an Old Time Music Hall.

Gran did not like the singing!

And there was a Glamorous Grandma Contest.

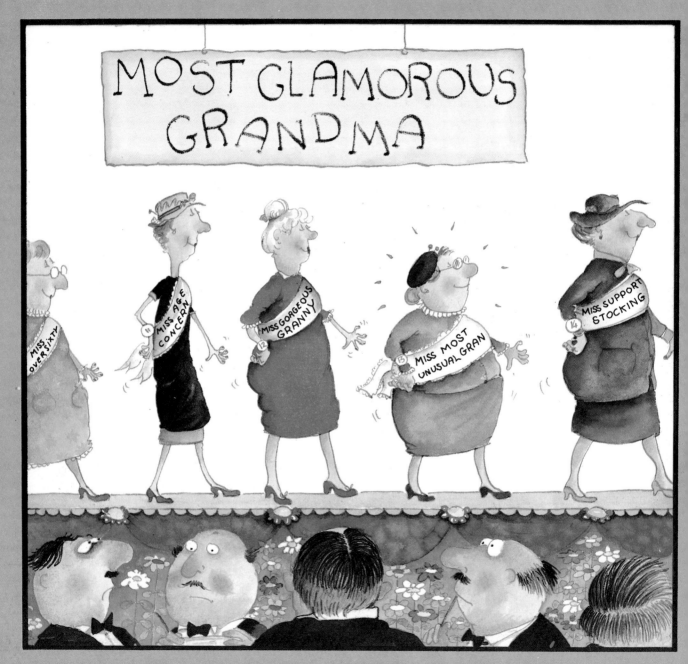

... Gran cheated of course!

She really
livened up
the fun fair!

We were asked to leave the amusement arcade!

On the Lunar Landscape Tour
Gran met some friends.

She took them to
the tea rooms!

So we missed the bus home.

Teacher blamed Gran!

"We've had enough of this dump!" said Gran.
"Fasten safety-belts!"

We zoomed towards Gran's planet . . .

and landed just in time
for carnival!

Gran did the Limbo . . .

. . . and climbed a bloomernut tree.

We were sad to leave,
but Gran had to get home
to feed the cat.

We landed in the
school playground
with a bump!

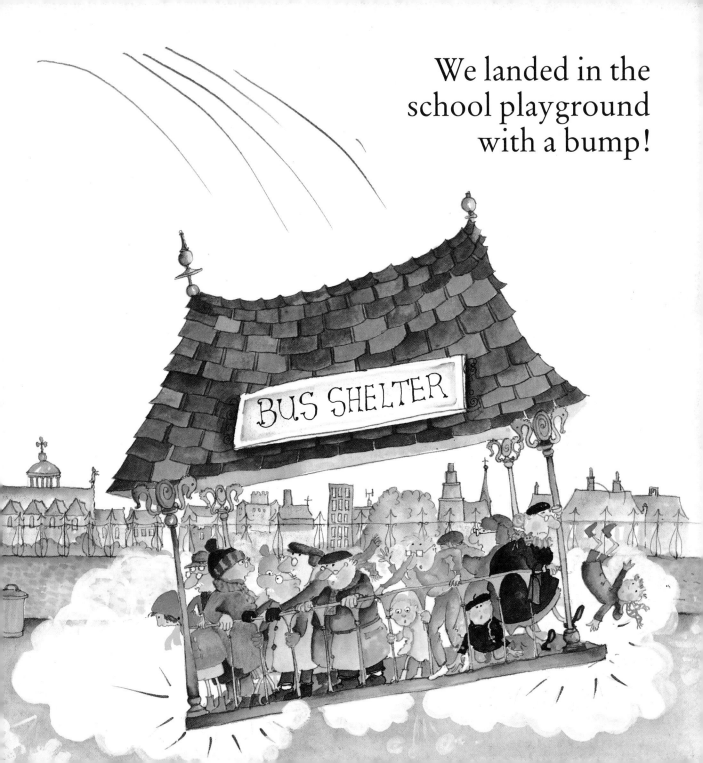

Mum and Dad marched Gran away.
"You're too old for that sort of thing now,"
they said.

"That's what they think," muttered Gran.

And when she got home she opened her own travel agency ...

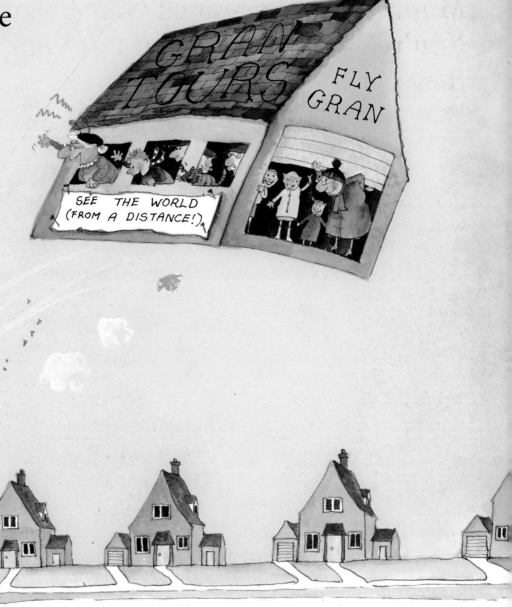

... in Dad's garage!

First published in Great Britain 1987
by William Heinemann Ltd
Published in Picture Lions 1988

Picture Lions is an imprint of the Children's Division,
part of Harper Collins Publishers,
8 Grafton Street, London W1X 3LA

Printed by Warners of Bourne and London